Cub's First Winter

by Rebecca Elliott

Licensed exclusively to Top That Publishing Ltd
Tide Mill Way, Woodbridge, Suffolk, IP12 1AP, UK
www.topthatpublishing.com
Copyright © 2010 Rebecca Elliott
All rights reserved
2 4 6 8 9 7 5 3
Manufactured in China

Written and illustrated by Rebecca Elliott

ISBN 978-1-78445-192-9

A catalogue record for this book is available from the British Library

'For Mum and Dad who have always taken such good care of their own cubs. x'

It was the first day of winter
and Cub could not sleep. 'OK,' said Mum.
'One more forest walk before bed. Come on ...'

'Why are all the trees undressed?' asked Cub.

'So that we can have
fun in the leaves!'
answered Mum.

And the snow clouds
gathered in the sky.

'Why are my friends asleep all the time?' asked Cub. 'Ssshhh! So that we can laugh at their snoring!' giggled Mum.

And the first snowflake fell to the ground.

'Why are the birds
going on holiday?' asked Cub.
'So they can tell us all about their
journey when they come back!' said Mum.

And the snow began to gently fall.

'Why is it so windy?' asked Cub.
'So that we can be blown about together
in the tall grass!' laughed Mum.

And the snow drifted down.

'Why can I see my own breath?' asked Cub.
'So that we can puff like steam trains!' puffed Mum.

And the snow began to settle on the ground.

'Why is the river solid?' asked Cub.
'So that we can slide and dance on it!' exclaimed Mum.

And the snow fell more quickly.

'Why does the sun disappear
so early?' asked Cub.
'So that we can look up at
the stars for longer,'
explained Mum.

And the snow got
deeper and deeper.

'Why is everything white?' asked Cub.

'Oh no!' gasped Mum.
'Quick, follow me before we lose our way home!'

And back they went through the white forest,
over the white river, up and down the white rocks
and round and round the white trees until,
at last, they found their way home!

'Why is it so c-c-cold?'
asked Cub.

'So that we can
snuggle up tight,'
whispered Mum,
with a smile.

'Why am I so tired?'
yawned Cub.
'Because it is sleepy time,'
murmured Mum.
'Night, night little cub.'